THE
Forgotten
CAROLS

THE Forgotten CAROLS

REVISED EDITION

A Christmas Story and Songs
MICHAEL MCLEAN

SHADOW MOUNTAIN
SALT LAKE CITY, UTAH

Visit us at shadowmountain.com

Library of Congress Cataloging-in-Publication Data

McLean, Michael, 1952-
  The forgotten carols / Michael Mclean.—Rev. ed.
     p.   cm.
  ISBN 1-59038-193-9 (pbk.)
  1. Jesus Christ—Nativity—Fiction. 2. Caregivers—Fiction.
  3. Aged men—Fiction. I. Title.
  PS3563.C3844 F67 2003
  813'.54—dc22
                                    2003014745

Printed in the United States of America   8006-7145
Banta, Menasha, WI

10 9 8 7 6 5 4 3 2 1

Contents

CHAPTER 1

My Name Is Constance

When her mother named her Constance, she had no intention of ever calling her Connie. Her mother once explained to her that Constance was a solid name, a name with substance and dignity, but "Connie," well, "Connie" was just fluff.

A lot of young girls growing up in her neighborhood would have welcomed a friendly "Hi, Connie" from their friends at school, or, at the very least, would have acknowledged the greeting with a smile. Not Constance. She corrected them resolutely. "My name is Constance," she would say, looking and sounding a bit like a stuffy old librarian. "I am *not* a Connie."

She had that right. She was not then nor did she ever plan to be a "Connie."

If it is possible to be obedient to a fault, Constance was. It never occurred to her that anything her mother ever said was not absolute truth. No advice, counsel, instruction, or observation her mother made was ever challenged. Constance tried in every way to be her mother in miniature. This remarkable devotion was an enormous source of pride for her mother, though Constance never knew it. All she knew was that her mother was never wrong.

That wasn't true of course. Her mother was wrong on just about everything that had anything to do with raising a healthy, well-adjusted, only child; she never encouraged her daughter to think or dream or feel or question or wonder or choose or discover anything for herself. She believed it was her job as the parent to control all that for her daughter—and Constance let her. But controlling her daughter's life never compensated Lillian Chamberlain for the loss of control of her own. World War II took her husband. Unsolicited diseases took her health. A letter of condolence from the president took her hope.

Though Constance was raised with precious little in the way of emotional nurturing, she received a more than adequate education (her mother's term) thanks to an inheritance left to her by the father she never knew. From the age of fourteen she had prepared herself for a practical career in nursing.

To fully appreciate what became of Constance you need to know that she had been a nurse at the Regional Hospital her entire career. Although she could never be accused of being overly compassionate, she had never shirked her duties or failed to follow a doctor's orders to the letter. And she had never, ever questioned or challenged anyone in authority at the hospital. Needless to say, doctors loved her—and patients didn't.

It was this absolute commitment to following the voice of authority that placed Constance in an extremely awkward position a few weeks before Christmas. The chief administrator of the hospital called her into his office with a special request.

"We have; . . ." Mr. Halifax paused, wanting to say this just right " . . . a special responsibility here at the hospital."

Constance sat up straighter in her chair.

"This community depends on us to help them when they need us. And to help them with the finest in hospital care requires what?"

Constance had learned in earlier private meetings with Mr. Halifax that he didn't really want her to answer these questions—it was just his way of communicating. She knew that what he really wanted was for her to act as if she had the answer on the tip of her tongue, and then he would take everything from there.

"That's right, Ms. Chamberlain; it requires money." As she had expected, he answered his own question. Then he continued, "And where does this money come from?

That's right, it comes from patients, or rather from insurance companies of patients. And what happens when there are difficulties collecting from these companies, Ms. Chamberlain? You were about to say that we have budget problems, and you're correct. And how do we overcome these budget shortfalls during these recessionary times? Well, we appeal to the very community we are trying to support; we give them a chance to help support us. Are you with me, Nurse Chamberlain?"

Few women would have tolerated such a patronizing tone, but Constance was not offended. In some ways, it reminded her of dinner conversations when she was growing up, and so, strangely, she felt right at home. She nodded her agreement much as she had most of her life.

"Then you're with me. Good! We have a wonderful opportunity to participate in a goodwill public relations effort that could benefit Regional Hospital enormously, and I need your help."

Then something rather odd happened. Mr. Halifax became very excited, like a little boy anticipating a huge gift at Christmas. She had never seen him quite like this before. Mr. Halifax went to his desk and lifted a telegram from a stack of papers.

"Listen to this!" He could hardly read it, he was so excited. "This comes from the chairman of the board of our parent company. It says, 'A prominent family has expressed interest in making a substantial contribution to the hospital in the new year. They are planning to take their holiday in Europe and will work out details of their gift when they return. They have an aging uncle whom they don't feel they can take with them for various reasons—psychological more than anything, I believe—and I told them we'd be happy to have one of our outstanding nurses care for him through the holidays. This is our opportunity to let the family know how committed we are to excellence in nursing care.'"

Mr. Halifax was almost emotional when he looked up from reading the telegram.

"Well, Nurse Chamberlain, there you have it. Straight from the chairman of the board. The schedule indicates that your wing, 3-East, is overstaffed this month, and, seeing as how you have no family constraints like so many others this time of year, I'd like you to handle this for me. Thank you."

He never really looked to see if she'd accepted the assignment. He simply handed her an address, a name, and a sketchy medical history. Before she could articulate a response, Mr. Halifax was shaking hands with his next appointment, and his secretary was ushering Constance out the door.

It wasn't in Constance's nature to defy the authority of Mr. Halifax, not to mention the chairman of the board. But just because she wouldn't have said no didn't mean she would have chosen, on her own, to say yes.

The assignment she'd just been given made her feel very uncomfortable. During her nurse's training, she'd had to work in every wing in the hospital for a week or two, and the only two experiences she had found unbearable were in the psychiatric ward and the maternity ward. Years before, she had written about those weeks in her journal with uncharacteristic candor: "I can't do the babies or the crazies. It's a good thing the nursing profession offers other

7

opportunities, or I fear I'd be forced to find another line of work."

The other thing Constance found uncomfortable was working outside the hospital itself. At Regional, everything was sterilized and safe. The patients would come and go, but the beds and the lamps and the furniture never changed. Although she'd read articles in trade publications about hospitals that were attracting patients with all sorts of "homey" interior decorating schemes, she was quite pleased that her hospital remained a stark, white, fully antiseptic environment. By working there, she felt like a real nurse. She wasn't certain she would be viewed as competent while nursing in someone's home.

There was some good news, however. With this assignment, she wouldn't have to be involved in all the Christmas activities that took place at the hospital. She had always thought them a nuisance, and so this December assignment would give her the perfect escape from what she considered the clutter of the holidays. *How bad can it be?* she thought as she rode the bus home from the hospital. *I'll avoid all those people tracking snow*

down the halls and singing out-of-tune carols. I'll miss those silly staff parties with the gag gifts everyone pretends are so funny. And for the first time in years, I won't have to deal with the season. I'll have only one man to baby-sit during the day, and the evenings will be mine—no shift work, no nights. Maybe this is what I've always wanted: a real Christmas vacation!

A faint smile came over her face as she thought about this respite from Christmas, not realizing that she was on the eve of the most memorable Christmas she would ever know.

CHAPTER 2

A Man Forgotten

Constance checked and double-checked, but there were no convenient bus routes to the address she would be attending for the next few weeks, and inasmuch as the hospital would be covering expenses, Constance took a taxi. Since the daily routine of her life had not required her to visit this part of town before, the closer she got to her destination, the more unfamiliar everything became.

The cab driver was not a chatty soul, for which Constance was grateful. She thought about asking him to pick her up at the end of her working day and possibly make this a routine for the next few weeks. But then it occurred to her that she might appear to be too forward, and that might encourage a familiarity she knew would make her uncomfortable—so she said nothing.

As the taxi began to slow down, her attention shifted from the new neighborhood she was entering to the fare on the meter in the cab, and she worried a bit about what kind of tip to give the driver. *Is it like tipping a waiter?* she wondered. *And if so, how does one judge the service in a taxi ride?* Since the cabby had driven safely and quietly, she decided to add 10 percent to the fare and ask for a receipt.

When she got out of the taxi and looked at the house she was about to enter, her first thought was, *So this is how the other half lives.* It was beautiful. Even though it was December, and a cold one at that, she could see that the expansive grounds around the place had been well manicured. Constance wasn't sure what size of house could rightly be called a mansion, but it occurred to her that this might be one. She walked slowly, not because she was afraid to enter, but because she was amazed that she was actually the one chosen to work here. Maybe Mr. Halifax believed she was more competent than she had ever realized.

She stood for a moment on the front porch, took a few deep breaths, and collected herself the way she always did before she entered the hospital to begin her shift. When she felt in control and competent she rang the front doorbell and waited. And waited. And waited.

She felt a hint of panic. Maybe she was at the wrong address. Maybe something had gone wrong inside. Maybe . . .

From behind her came a voice that startled her.

"It's not locked. Just open the door—and if you wouldn't mind, hold it for me, please."

She turned around and saw only a large, fresh-cut fir tree looking a bit like an evergreen missile rocketing toward her. She could see only the legs of whoever was propelling the tree and assumed they belonged to the voice she'd just heard. The tree showed no signs of slowing down as it approached the front door, and Constance was afraid that if she didn't open the door quickly, she might be run over. She pulled the storm door open and held it with her foot as she turned the oversized doorknob on the front door. At precisely the same moment she pushed the door open, she felt fresh Christmas-tree needles carrying her into the entry of the house.

Once inside, she maneuvered her way out of the clutches of the tree and spun free only long enough to watch the flash of green race on into another room. Like a magnet pulling her against her will, she followed the tree. When it stopped, so did she.

"Thanks! I didn't think I'd make it in without dropping it or breaking something," said the cheerful voice that had carried the tree. "Just make yourself at home and I'll be right back—got to wash the pine sap off my hands."

He disappeared into another room before the nurse got a good look at him. Now what was she supposed to do? Making herself at home wasn't something she knew how

14

to do very well in her own place, let alone someone else's. The branches on the evergreen were still bouncing a bit from all the activity, and, though Constance didn't notice, so was she.

The room she was standing in was from another world she'd never known nor ever even dreamed of. The high, arched ceiling and paneled walls were tastefully elegant without being opulent. The furnishings were antiques so perfectly suited to the home that they didn't draw attention to how valuable they must be. Where some rooms in houses that big and beautiful might intimidate their guests, this room made Constance feel, for the first time in her life, as if she were home. But after briefly indulging herself in this newfound warmth, her sense of professionalism, as she liked to think of it, caused her to dismiss her feelings.

"Hello!" said the carrier of the Christmas tree. "You must be the nurse from the hospital. I'm sorry no one was here to properly greet you, but the butler-housekeeper-valet-and-cook was out running some errands, and I wanted so much to get the tree up today, so I went

Christmas-tree shopping. It took longer than I'd planned to get this beauty, so I'm sorry I wasn't here to welcome you upon your prompt arrival. Please forgive me."

Who was this man? The nurse's mind began to race. He couldn't be the aging uncle mentioned in the telegram . . . could he?

He held out his hand. "Everyone calls me Uncle John."

Constance prided herself on never staring at anyone. It wasn't polite to stare. But she was, staring, and she couldn't help it. This must be—her patient! But he wasn't anything like what she'd imagined. He looked so . . . so . . . so normal. He wasn't the old geezer that she had dreamed about the past night—with saliva trickling from the corners of his mouth and hair growing out of his ears. He didn't have any ticks or affectations like those she'd seen in psychiatric patients years before. His eyes didn't have the faraway look she had prepared herself to deal with, and his clothes were beautifully coordinated and comfortably tailored. She couldn't have said why, but she had it in her mind that an older man with psychological problems would probably wear chest-high, polyester plaid pants, an ugly flannel shirt, slippers, and a ratty robe.

His hand was still extended, and finally she shook it. His grip was strong but gentle. Giving her hand a warm and reassuring squeeze, he held it a bit longer than she wanted so he could guide her eyes to his when he spoke to her. "You can call me Uncle John. And what shall I call you?"

"My name is Constance . . . Constance Louise Chamberlain." As the words left her mouth, she realized she'd made a mistake. Her personal professional code demanded that she be friendly but never familiar, and here she was, right off the bat, sharing her first, last, and middle names, which she gave only when she had to on official printed material.

"Constance, eh? Well you certainly *look* like a Constance. But don't feel bad. I can see beyond that, and I believe that all people can re-create themselves if they know where to turn for help. I'll call you Connie Lou."

If real life had background music the way movies do,

right then you would have heard the kind of music they play when the gunfight is about to begin. Constance's blood was running cold. He had touched a nerve, and she was straining to keep herself in check. How dare he be so critical and so familiar! After all, if anyone needed "re-creating," it would certainly be him. *He* was the patient. *He* was the one with psychological problems.

She recognized that she was losing her professional distance, so she tried to calm herself down before responding. The fact that he was still holding her hand didn't make things any easier.

"I'm sorry I didn't introduce myself properly in the beginning. Why don't we just call me Nurse Chamberlain or Ms. Chamberlain?"

She was proud of herself for setting things straight so gracefully and for not losing control.

"Well, whenever 'we' call you anything, 'we'll' make sure it's either Nurse Chamberlain or Ms. Chamberlain, but as for me, I'm going to call you Connie Lou. You see, if I call you Nurse or Ms. or something equally distant

and lonely, that's all you'll ever be to me. But Connie Lou
. . . ah, there's someone worth getting to know."

Constance wasn't weighing her words anymore. "Sir,
this is not a date we're on here. I am a professional, and I
don't believe I like the idea of a patient of mine calling
me Connie Lou."

Uncle John's eyes always sparkled, but the gleam
seemed to turn up a notch with each exchange in their
conversation. He thought for a moment and then replied,
"You're right. It's not fair that I tell you what you can call
me and then turn around and tell you what I'll call you."

The nurse didn't think it was visible, but her patient
could see the hint of a sigh—part relief, part victory.
Then, when she was confident that the matter was
settled, her patient said, "You don't have to call me Uncle
John just because everyone else does. Call me whatever
you like. And I'll call you Connie Lou."

The background music no one could hear had
changed from dueling drama to comic farce. Constance
Louise Chamberlain recognized what should have been
obvious before she got there: this was all a game for this

man, and she couldn't take anything he said or did personally. She was dealing with someone who obviously wasn't in his right mind or else he wouldn't need a nurse to stay with him. She decided that for the good of Regional Hospital, and for the sake of the much-needed gift this patient's family might bring when they returned from Europe, she should play along as best she could.

"Very well, then," Constance said with a smile born of inner resolve and confidence that she was handling the situation properly, "I'll call you John or Uncle John if you like. Perhaps we could sit quietly here and get better acquainted."

"That's the spirit, Connie Lou." Uncle John motioned for Constance to be seated first, and then he joined her.

"What can I tell you about me that you don't already know?" John asked while looking directly at the medical chart the nurse had created for him the night before. "Tell me something, Connie Lou. Do I look crazy to you? I mean, really? Wouldn't a crazy person be wearing something like . . . like . . . like chest-high polyester plaid pants, an ugly flannel shirt, slippers, and a ratty robe?"

How did he know? How could he *possibly* have known something she'd never told another soul in her life? She'd only thought it, and very privately at that. This was eerie. Constance shook her head and decided it had to be a coincidence because the alternative was unthinkable.

"No, John, you don't look crazy to me. But then, I've never been a good judge of crazy people."

"Who has?" he responded. "The Marquis de Sade?" John couldn't help but chuckle at his own joke. He half hoped that his nurse would get it and join him, but she didn't.

The little attempt at humor hadn't warmed up Constance at all as far as John could see, so he pulled back and let her take things at her own pace. In due time, she asked John a question in a voice he recognized as the voice people use to sound professional and dignified.

"Why do you believe people think you're crazy, John?"

"Because I tell the truth," he said. "And in a world where things false and temporary are worshipped and adored, it's easier to dismiss as crazy those who tell the truth than it is to pay the price of sincerely listening to what they have to say."

He said this with no bitterness or disdain for the world his words reproached but with genuine love mingled with sadness.

Before she had a chance to ask any more questions, John stood up, excused himself for a moment, and left the room. When he returned, he was carrying what looked like a very old, relatively small valise fashioned from leather straps and carved wood. Constance had never seen anything else like it, and she was so preoccupied with the case itself that she didn't ask the question Uncle John was waiting for her to ask.

"Don't you want to know what's in here?" he asked with childlike enthusiasm. When she didn't immediately answer, he added, "These are the most precious possessions I have on earth. These are my Christmas ornaments!"

Christmas ornaments? The man's most precious possessions were the Christmas ornaments he carried around in an antique suitcase? For Constance, this was evidence enough that her patient belonged in a sanitarium.

As if he were preparing the room for someone's arrival, Uncle John went on and on about the ornaments. Each one, he claimed, had a story behind it that he told and retold every Christmas as he placed it on the tree.

As he carried on about the contents of his still-unopened suitcase, Constance had an odd thought—particularly for someone who never cared much for the folderol of putting up and taking down Christmas decorations. She thought to herself, *There can't possibly be enough ornaments in that suitcase to trim this enormous tree. Maybe he's got another box he'll bring in later.*

Strangely, Constance had become so caught up in her thoughts about the ornaments and the tree that she found herself interrupting John to ask him about the other decorations.

"Oh, this is all of them," he told her, patting the suitcase.

"Everything you need to trim this big tree is in that suitcase?" she asked incredulously.

"That's right."

"Then you *are* crazy!"

John wanted to hug her, but he was afraid she'd misunderstand, so instead he gave her his warmest smile and said, "Connie Lou, we're going to get along just fine."

The opening of the ancient ornament case was a ritual of sorts for Uncle John. He carefully unlatched the cracked leather straps that held the case closed. With each slow and deliberate motion, he seemed to be reliving a memory that was deep and sweet. As he drifted back to other places and other times, he gave life to his memories by humming something to himself. It was a melody Constance didn't recognize.

Then, as if someone had tapped him on the shoulder, he returned from his daydream, looked directly at Constance, grinned, and raised his eyebrows expectantly. Then he proudly opened the case. After quickly checking to make sure nothing was damaged, he displayed his treasure for Constance to see.

As the case was opened, Constance felt something like a breath of spring enter the room. She couldn't deny it, though part of her wanted to. And she couldn't deny the little-girl anticipation she felt either. Constance was unfamiliar with this feeling. She had been raised in a home where surprises were avoided at all costs. All gifts, though wrapped, were practical and known in advance. All her days were scheduled, and all her activities were thoroughly planned. Even in her nursing, a profession filled with the unexpected, she was rarely surprised because she so meticulously prepared herself for every conceivable medical problem she might face. Because her career was her life, she even spent time on the bus to the hospital each day quietly rehearsing what she'd say during the obligatory small talk with other nurses and doctors. But she was *not* in the hospital now, and she was *not* in her mother's home now, and she was *not* caring for someone for whom she could have prepared herself, and so a part of her surrendered. For the first time in her life, Constance Louise Chamberlain surrendered to the simple joy of wonder.

At first glance, the only thing in John's yuletide treasure chest that reminded Constance of a Christmas

25

ornament was the star that virtually filled the left half of the opened suitcase. The other objects were an eclectic combination of unusual, beautiful, common, foreign, and old things that all made her wonder. Where had they come from; what did they mean?

Uncle John's eyes went back and forth between his ornaments and his nurse. He would watch her eyes and guess which piece she was looking at, and then he'd quietly gaze at one with her. This went on for some time with John continuing to hum unfamiliar tunes.

"Which one goes on the tree first?" she wondered out loud.

"This one," he answered without hesitation. He then carefully lifted from the case something that resembled an arched entrance or passageway made of stone. John placed it in the nurse's hands so she could examine it more closely.

It was fascinating. It made her think of the kind of doorway people must have entered in ancient times. It seemed made of real stones and mortar. Small as it was, it had been crafted with great attention to detail. A thick piece of cloth hung where Constance expected to see a door. She asked John about it.

"Thousands of years ago, it was common to place heavy woven pieces over entrances to serve as doors," he said, sounding as though he knew what he was talking about.

Then Constance's eyes focused on something that had been painted on the stones above the entrance. It looked as though it had been written long ago, in a language she could not read.

"I made this myself," John said proudly. "It's a replica of the entrance to the inn where there was no room for Joseph and Mary. This piece always goes on the tree first."

Constance took that as her cue to place the ornament on the tree. "Where would you like me to place it?" she asked.

"We have to sing first," he answered.

Sing what? she wondered. "*O Little Town of Bethlehem*" *or* "*Silent Night*"? John read her thoughts.

"No, no, no, Connie Lou. Not those. We'll sing the forgotten carols."

She turned from her study of the ornament in her hand and gave John a quizzical expression. "The what?" she asked.

"The forgotten carols. That's what I call them anyway. The carols about characters who played supporting roles in the Christmas story, who have either been forgotten, overlooked, misunderstood, or ignored."

"How did you find these carols?" she questioned.

"To tell you the truth, Connie Lou, they kind of found me. Take the innkeeper, for example. There was a man who turned away Joseph and Mary—not because he was mean or thoughtless. He was just taking care of business. What haunted him, though, was the feeling that he hadn't really done all he could have for the pregnant woman and her husband."

"How do you know that?" Constance asked, hoping for an answer that made sense.

"He told me," was his reply.

Sure, she thought. *That makes sense. If you're insane!*

"What do you mean, 'He told you'?" Constance felt like getting tough. She wasn't going to get drawn any further into such nonsense.

"He just told me. It was several years after it had happened. I had returned to Bethlehem on a sort of pilgrimage I made celebrating the birth, and I spent the night in his inn. We began talking, and the subject came up. Then, when he found out who I was, he told me his story."

John sat at the piano and began to play. He played with great feeling. But then, Constance never believed disturbed people were incapable of feeling—her studies had taught her that in many psychiatric cases the feelings are simply misdirected. She thought that if there was ever living proof of that, Uncle John was it.

Closing his eyes so that he would accurately reflect the spirit of the innkeeper as he remembered it, he began to sing:

I am a man forgotten; no one recalls my name.
And thousands of years will fail to fully erase the shame.
But I turned a profit nicely that day
That I turned the couple away . . . I turned them away.

John's voice was hypnotic. He evoked each phrase with such a strong sense of feeling that whether you liked his voice or not, you had to listen.

I didn't sleep that evening, though I'd sold out my place.
Somehow I felt uneasy . . . something about her face.
Why did I wish that I'd let them stay?
I don't think they could have paid . . .
Or could they have paid?

Restless I left my bedroom.
I walked the streets all night,
Lost in the world I lived in.
Then found by a heavenly light!
Staring at one bright star in the sky,
I heard a baby cry.

I knew where the cry had come from
'Cause I'd told them where to go,
But I didn't think I could face them,
And so I walked slowly home,
Missing my chance to share in the joy.
I never saw her boy.

He never would condemn me.
I did that all on my own.

He offered His forgiveness,
And ever since then I've known
He lets us choose each hour of each day,
If we'll let Him in to stay.

Let Him in . . . let Him in . . .
Let the hope and joy begin.
Let Him in . . . let Him in . . .
Let the peace on earth begin.
Whether it be in your world today
Or a crowded Bethlehem inn,
Find a way . . . make Him room . . . let Him in.

When the singing of the first forgotten carol was over, Uncle John rose from the piano, took Constance by the hand, and walked over to the bare Christmas tree. He pointed to a place on the tree that he found worthy of this ornament. He called the spot the "heart of the tree." Constance hung the ornament far enough in on the evergreen branch that there was no danger of it accidentally falling off. And as she did, she noticed again the strange writing across the top of the ornament. John read her thoughts and answered, "That was the inscription written by the innkeeper over the entrance to his inn shortly before he died. I wanted to preserve it on the ornament just the way my friend had written it. It says: 'Let Him In.'"

Before excusing himself to take a nap, Uncle John showed Constance around the main floor of the house. He wanted her to be comfortable, though he knew such a thing was difficult for her. He explained that the butler, who while the family was away also served as the house-keeper, valet, and cook, would be working around the house and that she should not be alarmed when she heard him come in the back way. Uncle John also mentioned that the butler was shy and probably wouldn't say much, but that she would be a fool to pass up his egg salad sandwiches on rye, were he to offer her some.

Uncle John reminded her that she was free to leave at five o'clock and asked her not to wake him to say good-bye. He also requested that she leave her phone number on the pad by the telephone in the hall so the butler could call her in the event of an emergency. Then he climbed the long staircase and was gone.

The rest of the afternoon passed rather uneventfully.

She heard the butler come in, but the only glimpse she caught of him was when she went into the kitchen to get a drink of water. From what she could tell, which wasn't much, he was about the same size as Uncle John, with a bit of a belly, a full beard, and very thick glasses.

At the stroke of five, she called a cab and prepared to go home. Although she'd never given out her home phone number to a man of any age, she felt relatively safe in leaving her number on the pad by the phone as she'd been asked. Her patient was obviously suffering from bouts of delusion, but if today proved anything, it was that he was perfectly harmless.

CHAPTER 3

Homeless

About ten minutes past five o'clock, the cab arrived. When Constance told the driver her address, he surprised her by asking which route she preferred, "E" Street or Charleston Avenue? She didn't want him to know how unfamiliar she was with the area, but her long hesitation gave her away. Trying to disguise her indecision, she suggested he take the route with the least rush-hour traffic.

Five minutes later, the knot Constance usually felt in her stomach when she was in unfamiliar territory began to tighten. She was in the heart of the homeless section of town when the traffic slowed to a snail's pace. Ahead she could see the flashing emergency lights of an ambulance and a police car.

Instinctively the nurse told the cab driver to pull over to the side of the road and wait for her. As a professional nurse, she felt it her duty to offer assistance at the scene of an accident. As she approached the flashing lights, she took a few deep breaths and introduced herself to the nearest police officer.

"Excuse me. I'm a nurse at Regional Hospital. Can I be of any assistance?"

"Thanks for offering, but it looks like the paramedics have things under control."

"What happened?"

"A minor accident. They think the driver may have broken his collarbone, but that's about all. Fortunately no one else was hurt. Excuse me." The officer then began clearing the crowd and working to direct traffic around the accident.

On the walk back to the taxi, Constance noticed the mattresses in the alleys and the cardboard shelters leaned against the side of old buildings. *People actually live here,* she thought, and she wondered how many of them were sick or would soon become sick in such conditions.

Although she'd seen homeless people at the hospital before and had treated several, she felt something that was absent in her hospital work as she walked along the street where these people were trying to survive.

As she crossed the last side street before reaching her taxi, she heard some street singing. A group was huddled around a fire they had built in an old metal garbage can spray painted like a Christmas tree. They sang a bittersweet Christmas song that Constance had never heard before:

> *Homeless, homeless*
> *Like the Christ child was . . . we are*
> *Homeless, homeless,*
> *But there is hope because*
> *He came down to earth to lead us,*

And He vowed He'd never leave us
Homeless, homeless,
For in His love there is a home.

The song had captured her attention, but the singing of it, with such hope and optimism, was capturing her heart.

Homeless, homeless
Was His humble birth.
Homeless, homeless,
And still He changed the earth.
Nothing kept His heart from giving
Though most of His life was living
Homeless, homeless.
He showed it's how we live,
Not where.
And when His homeless days on earth were done,
He went home to where we all came from.
And He went to prepare
A mansion for us there.
He gave His whole life to lead us,
And I know He'll never leave us
Homeless, homeless,
For in His love there is a home.

As she pulled herself away from this unlikely group of Christmas carolers, she was struck by how much she wanted to give them something—some money, a hand-out—but no one asked. Here, of all places, she would have expected panhandlers and beggars, but instead she found dignity and hope. *Where had it come from,* she wondered as the taxi drove her home. *Where had it come from?*

After supper and before calling it a day, she thought she'd read awhile. She tried to get into her routine of studying from nursing journals and medical books, but for some reason, that was impossible. Then she tried to do some casual reading, but nothing she read was anywhere near as interesting as her own reflections on the day. Later, while she was getting ready for bed, she detected the same sense of anticipation she'd felt earlier that day. But she didn't fight it. And while she brushed out her hair, she found herself humming tunes that until today she'd never heard before.

CHAPTER 4

You Were Not There in Bethlehem

The next day at the mansion, Constance was greeted at the door by the butler. *Greeted* is probably the wrong word; he didn't say anything to her that she could properly understand. After opening the door for her, he mumbled something and went upstairs. *He must be going to announce my arrival to Uncle John*, she thought.

She hung her coat and scarf in the hall closet and

found a comfortable chair in the main room and waited. Then she heard a clear, thin sound coming from upstairs. It sounded like a wooden flute of some kind. The melody was hypnotic, but the actual sound of the instrument was even more so.

As the sound got closer, she expected any moment to see Uncle John coming down the stairs playing whatever instrument was making that remarkable sound. What she didn't expect to see was her patient dressed like a shepherd who might have lived at the time of Christ.

The clothes he was wearing were as remarkable as the sound he'd been making. To say that he looked as though he'd just walked out of the movie *Ben Hur* would be an insult, really, because he looked more authentic than anything ever portrayed in a film. His entrance was so convincing that for a moment Constance didn't just think he *looked* like a shepherd from Judea's hills, but that he *was* one.

But reality soon came into focus for the professional nurse. And when it did, she didn't know whether to be concerned for her patient's behavior or amused by it. Contrary to her nature, she chose the latter.

As he played his haunting tune, he circled his nurse a few times and then motioned her to follow him, Pied-Piper style. She did, and he guided her to the opened case of Christmas ornaments. Continuing to play the music, he nodded his head toward the ornaments, hoping that Constance would read his thoughts. Strangely enough, she did.

She saw a beautiful miniature shepherd's flute like the one John was playing, and she picked it up. It was a remarkable likeness, with tiny wooden reeds cut and shaped to look like an ancient instrument. John continued to play for her while she examined the ornament, and then he marched her toward the Christmas tree. Not wanting to stop playing so he could speak, he used his eyes and head movement to indicate she was to place the little flute on the tree.

Constance thought she was playing along beautifully and had reached to hang the ornament on the tree when suddenly John's flute-playing sounded like a swarming

43

hive of angry bees. Constance felt a surge of panic and almost dropped the little flute. *What was wrong? What was happening? Was he having a seizure? What should she do?*

The state of emergency she was preparing in her mind to handle didn't last long, however. John took the flute away from his lips long enough to say, "Not so close to the other ornament, Connie Lou. It's a big tree." When he could see that Constance knew what he meant, he went on playing.

Constance decided to hold the miniature flute in a general area of the tree and see if the location met with the shepherd's approval before committing herself to hanging the ornament. She first held it in a space directly below the only other ornament on the tree, and then she looked to John. He gave her a "so-so" back-and-forth nod and played a mediocre note over and over again. She decided to try another spot much higher and to the right. Victory! The music soared, and she knew she'd found the spot. As she hung the little flute, her back was to John, so he didn't see her smile from its beginning, but as she turned around he caught the last of it, and it was beautiful.

When the musical phrase he was playing came to a natural pause, he began to sing:

> *The flock was more than peaceful.*
> *The night was dark and deep.*
> *The stillness wrapped around me,*
> *And I drifted off to sleep.*
> *And when my friends awoke me,*
> *Oh, what a tale they had to tell!*

Between verses he played his flute.

> *They said the angels told them*
> *About the newborn king.*
> *They had a star to guide them,*
> *They heard the heavens sing.*
> *They said that when they found Him,*
> *They knew they'd never be the same.*

Again he played an interlude before singing the carol's first chorus.

> *Somehow I did believe them*
> *Though everything I knew*
> *Said I should not believe them.*

45

This story can't be true.
But there was something magic in the air
That made me feel as if I had been there.

The rhythm of the song, the theme, everything about it was different from anything Constance thought of as "Christmas music," but it was doing the very thing her past Christmases had failed to do—it was moving her heart.

I asked a thousand questions.
Their answers startled me.
The more I heard, the more I thought,
I knew this could not be.
And then the struggle started—
My head was wrestling with my heart.
Why would a God from heaven
Come to the world this way?
Why in a lowly stable
Would the Messiah lay?
I shook my head and asked them
To tell the story one more time.

And, yes, I did believe them
Though I'd not seen a thing.
I did not go to Bethlehem

Or hear the angels sing,
But there was something magic in the air
That made me feel as if I had been there.
I knew that as the world
Moves on through time,
There would be more stories just like mine
About the souls who've chosen to believe
In something that they never got to see.

And do you think you'll join us
Though you've not seen a thing?
You were not there in Bethlehem
To hear the angels sing.
But if you feel the spirit in the air,
Then, just like me, you'll know that
He was here . . . He was here.
The King of kings and Lord of lords was here,
He was here . . . He was here.
And He will come again, for He was here.

As John repeated the chorus, he became more and more emotional. It was as if he had to make sure Constance knew what he knew.

Constance had seen evangelical preachers on television before and always felt uncomfortable when they became emotional. She thought their tears were nothing but a sham—a dramatic ploy staged to get more money. But what she was feeling at that moment with John was completely different. As a nurse, she had seen men cry from pain, but in her whole life she'd never been around a man who cried sweet tears of spiritual gratitude and joy. She felt something welling up inside, and she knew she had to resist it—push it back down to where it came from. First of all, she had never cried in front of anyone, and she couldn't let that happen now—certainly not in front of a patient. But her greater concern was that she didn't know what it was that she was feeling.

Perhaps it was the magic in the air.

Uncle John took Constance's hand and walked her over to the sofa, where he sat her down.

"Thank you," he said gratefully, "for letting me share that with you. I love that shepherd."

Sitting next to John gave her a chance to feel the fabric of his costume against her skin. "Where did you get this material?" she asked. "I've never seen anything like it."

"This was his, actually. He told me that he wanted me to have it so I'd never forget his story. I never have, and on the day I place his ornament on the tree, I wear his clothes to honor him."

Constance wondered what had happened to Uncle John in his life to create in him the need for these fantasies. Even though she was not skilled in clinical psychology, she tried to remember her college courses on the subject. She dared to ask Uncle John a few questions, hoping the answers would give her a clearer insight into his kind of mental illness.

"Your friend, this . . . this shepherd. When did you first get to know this man?" she asked.

"About A.D. 42, I believe," he said, straining to remember.

"So what's become of him?" she asked.

John paused.

"He's dead, Connie Lou."

"Of course. But what about you, John?"

Her patient pinched himself and smiled.

"I'm not," he said brightly.

"But you've lived all this time since then. Is that right?"

"That's right."

"Don't you think that's a little unusual?" she probed.

"A *little*? It's absolutely *incredible!* How many people do you know who have been around as long as I have?"

His response to her question surprised her.

"How long do you think you've been around, John?"

"Oh, it's getting close to two thousand years." After a moment he nodded to himself that his estimate was correct and then continued. "I'd say that's more than a little unusual, wouldn't you, Connie Lou?"

"I'd say it's unbelievable."

"Well, of course it's unbelievable. If it hadn't happened to me, I'd have a hard time believing it myself."

"How did it happen that you have been alive all this time?"

John's expression grew a bit more serious. Constance thought she might have hit a nerve, and so she watched him carefully. She had learned in her psychology studies that body language clues can be very telling.

"I can't tell you," he finally said.

"You can't tell me because you don't want to or because you don't really know how it happened?" Constance felt very good about her question.

"You wouldn't understand—not now, anyway—so let's just leave it at that." John stood up. Constance immediately recognized his standing as the body-language clue she had been looking for. John was obviously uncomfortable talking about this and wanted to escape, but she wasn't about to let him.

"What are you running away from, John?"

He looked puzzled at her question. Constance took his look as more evidence that she was on to something. She persisted.

"What are you running away from?"

"I'm not running away from anything."

"Oh yes you are," she asserted.

"No I'm *not!*" he fired back.

"Then why did you stand up just now?" she said knowingly.

"*Because old shepherd clothes itch!* I'm going to change." He walked out of the room, leaving his psychologist to read that body language any way she wished.

CHAPTER 5

A Voice That Cannot Sing

$\mathcal{C}$onstance decided that she would have to back off for a while. She'd find ways to get to the root of his psychosis if she were patient, she believed. She'd become his friend . . . an ally . . . and then when he felt safe with her, he'd share the innermost feelings of his soul, and she would bring him triumphantly out of the world of his delusions into the world of reality.

She was imagining what that would be like—to change someone's life. How proud her mother would have to be of her. How proud she would feel of herself! She savored these feelings for quite a while.

Then, awkwardly crashing through the swinging door that led to the kitchen, came the butler with a silver tray full of food and two glasses of juice. He practically dropped the tray on the coffee table near the sofa where she sat, and, as he walked back toward the kitchen, she heard him mumble, "Egg salad on rye."

The sandwiches did look good, and John had told her she'd be foolish to pass them up, but she didn't know whether to wait for John or to go ahead. While she was trying to decide what to do, she heard Uncle John's voice come from upstairs.

"Are those egg salad sandwiches on rye I smell? Connie Lou, you go ahead and get started. I'll be right down."

Constance took one of the half sandwiches and sniffed it before taking a bite. She'd never noticed egg salad to have much of an aroma at all. *John must have a keen sense of smell*, she thought and then she took a bite. Ambrosia! Uncle John was right. Anyone who passed these up *was* a fool.

Uncle John joined her, dressed as he had been the day before, and he looked comfortable. As they ate, they both commented on what a treat the food was, and when they finished, Uncle John announced, "Time we do another ornament."

From his special case of Christmas ornaments he selected one that looked like a very old writing tool. When John presented it to Constance for her inspection, she could see the ink stains still on the tip.

When she handed the pen back to John, he walked it over to the tree and was about to place it there with the other two ornaments when something shocked Constance. A thought seized her brain and made her captive to its wishes. She quietly raced to the piano and began pounding on the keys with reckless abandon. When Uncle John's head spun around to see what was the matter, she saw in his eyes a kind of bewildered panic.

55

"Connie Lou, what's wrong?" John raced to her side as she collapsed on the keyboard.

"What's the matter, Connie? What do you need?" John tried to help her to her feet.

She couldn't be moved. "Not so close . . . not so close."

John backed off to give her room to breathe.

When she had his complete, anxiety-filled attention, with grand dramatic effect she said, "Not so close to the other ornament, Uncle John. It's a really *big* tree!"

Her laughter started as a mischievous little chuckle that emanated from her brain. Then it swept through her body like a fire that hit full strength in her stomach, and before she could contain it, she was laughing uncontrollably. It was contagious. John began laughing a bit himself at the joke she had played on him, but it grew to his own belly laugh simply because his nurse was laughing so crazily. She tried so hard to stop, but just when she would think she had herself under control, another wave of laughter would overcome her. Tears came to her eyes, and her sides ached. It was as if all the laughter of a lifetime were being released in one afternoon.

She had not planned it, rehearsed it, or even thought about it. It had just happened, and it marked her second great surrender in as many days—to the innocent joy of laughter.

When the laughter finally died down, Constance braced herself for the wave of embarrassment she expected. But it never came. Maybe it was the environment, maybe it was the season, maybe it was her patient who made her feel safe somehow. She didn't know why, but she felt that an enormous weight had been lifted from her shoulders, and she was renewed.

Uncle John still had the pen in his hand, and he took it with him to the piano. He placed it as a source of inspiration on the piano's music stand and then began to play. The music would underscore the story he was about to tell.

"Connie Lou, I want to tell you about this pen. I received it from a man who told me his story late one evening many Christmases ago.

"We were talking about inspiration—where it comes from, why it comes, how it changes us. And he spoke of a time when he felt completely uninspired, without direction, lost. And then he had a dream.

"'In my dream,' he told me, 'I was a very young angel in a very heavenly place when a trumpet was sounded and an announcement made. All the angels in heaven were invited to audition for the choir that would announce the Holy Birth. The excitement and anticipation caused my little angel heart almost to burst.

"'When my moment arrived, I stood before the musical tribunal and sang . . . and sang . . . and sang. No one interrupted or snickered at me because, well, this was heaven. But I knew immediately that I would not be invited to join the choir for one obvious reason: I—couldn't sing. I felt the music, but I couldn't get that feeling to come into my voice.

"'The Grand Chorus Master smiled and nodded to his chief assistant to show me out. "This isn't fair," I pleaded. "If you could hear what is in my heart, you'd let me sing." I ran back toward the Chorus Master and begged him to give me another chance. And as I did, music began to fill the room. And I recognized it, for it was the music coming directly from my tender, innocent heart.'"

As John played the young angel's forgotten carol, Constance heard instruments from an orchestra—faint at first, then loud enough to be in the room with them. And then she heard a choir singing glorious alleluias. How could that be? Where was the sound coming from? Was her patient's psychosis contagious? Had she been seduced into his delusions?

She had nowhere to turn for answers, and so she surrendered to the music, and it filled her in ways the answers she was seeking never could.

Then, with full orchestral underscore, John completed his story: "'All the other angels stood motionless and amazed as they heard the sound, and when my carol to my King was over, the Grand Chorus Master stood.

"'"Oh little one," he said, "you have so much to give, and your time will come."

"'"Then I can't sing with the choir?" I looked for him to change his mind, but he only shook his head and smiled.

"'"You have a different voice, but it *will* be heard. Centuries from now it will be heard. More orchestras and choirs than you can now imagine will be giving the music of your heart a voice that will echo through time."'"

As John played the final strains of this forgotten carol's melody, Constance heard a descant from the unseen orchestra. She recognized the countermelody as "Joy to the World," which turned into the "Hallelujah Chorus" and ended as the finale from "For unto Us a Child Is Born."

"It was *Handel?*" Constance exclaimed. "This is the pen of George Frideric Handel?"

"The one he wrote *Messiah* with," John clarified.

"I can't believe it," she said.

"No," John corrected her, "you *won't* believe it. There's a big difference."

"What do you mean?" she said a little defensively.

"You made up your mind a long time ago that something like this could never happen, and so you've chosen not to believe it could be true."

"But it doesn't make any sense," Constance argued.

"Why doesn't it?" he asked.

"Because things like that just don't happen." She was getting angry.

"Says who?"

"Says my mother!" She couldn't stop the words from spilling out of her mouth. And when she said them, she sounded just like the schoolgirl she once was. She knew that John could have had a field day with a response like that. She was waiting for him to tease her the way the children at school used to do. But instead of attacking, he retreated.

"Connie Lou, I'm sorry. You don't have to believe me. There's nothing wrong with you because you can't believe me. The most natural thing in the world is to question things and want to know why. You haven't failed. You haven't done anything wrong. You're my friend, and I apologize for sounding as though I was judging you. Please forgive me."

No one had ever asked for Constance's forgiveness before, so she wasn't sure how to give it. And no one had ever told her before that she was all right. People had told her she was competent, but until this moment, she'd never been told that, as she was, she was all right. She'd never been told it was fine to feel and question and challenge and disagree with an adult. She'd never been treated like this before, and so she didn't know how to react.

Uncle John then took the pen that he claimed once belonged to Handel, and he dipped it into a little ink bottle that was in the ornament case. He then wrote something on a piece of paper, blew the fresh ink dry, and handed the paper to Constance. Before she could read it, he told her it was time for his nap, and he left the room.

His note read:

Connie Lou,

I'm afraid you're stuck with me, and I hope you will learn to like me someday, because you can't make me not like you.

John

Constance held the note written with the same pen that supposedly had written the glorious music of Handel's *Messiah*. She still couldn't believe it had, but she could believe one thing: today it had written something beautiful.

CHAPTER 6

Mary Let Me Hold Her Baby

It started snowing that afternoon, and Constance found herself drawn to the overstuffed chair by the window so she could watch. Although she had a great deal on her mind, the falling snow gave her an excuse to think about nothing for a while. It was a soft and gentle snow, the kind that brings quiet. As she sank into the deep, goose-down cushions of her chair, she gazed out the window and watched the ground become a thick, white carpet. The butler bumbled into the room and lit a fire in the fireplace, but she barely noticed. The world became soft and peaceful and safe and warm, and she hoped nothing would disturb her for a while.

Through the lace curtain of falling snow, she saw some children starting to build a snowman. Among them was an older woman who looked as if she was having as much fun as the children were. Constance was amazed that a woman that old could be so childlike, so carefree, so . . . so much fun. Constance wondered if the woman might be the children's grandmother.

"What a wonderful surprise. It's Sarah!" Had John not spoken, Constance would not have noticed that he had entered the room. He tapped on the window and tried to get the attention of the woman playing in the snow with the children.

"Oh, Connie Lou, you have to meet her," he said enthusiastically. Then he opened the window and called, "Sarah! Sarah! Come in out of the cold."

The old woman was helping the children place the head on the snowman. "In a minute, John, in a minute."

"You're going to adore this woman, Connie Lou," Uncle John said confidently. "Everybody does. She's one of my favorite forgotten carols."

"She's *what?*" Constance said, sitting up on the edge of her chair.

Uncle John greeted Sarah at the door with a warm embrace, and he walked her to the fire.

"Connie Lou, this is my dear friend Sarah. Sarah, this is my nurse and new friend, Connie Lou Chamberlain."

Constance stood and went over to shake hands. "My name is Constance. I'm really not a Connie," she said out of habit.

John turned his head so Sarah couldn't see him whisper to his nurse, "Give it a rest. She's my friend. Try to be nice."

Connie Lou did her best.

"So, Sarah. Tell me. How long have you and John been friends?"

"Forever," Sarah answered, and then she smiled at

John. "Well, not exactly forever. It just seems that long. What's it really been, John? About nineteen hundred years?"

Constance shrieked inside, *Oh, no! They're coming to get me!* But after a few seconds, she managed to calm herself enough to ask a few more questions.

"What brings you to this part of . . . of . . . the planet?" Constance didn't know what else to say.

"I try to look John up every few hundred years to see if he still remembers me—and if he remembers my carol."

John smiled at his old friend. "I remember, Sarah. I always remember." Then something very curious happened. John went to his ornament case and pulled out something Constance had no idea was there: a large square of soft cloth. "Swaddling clothes," he said. And when he handed them to Sarah, she held them as if she were holding a baby. John explained to his nurse that his friend Sarah had a remarkable gift. "She had a way with children, Connie, and she molded them like clay. She found the greatness in them all and she nurtured it each day. Though she never had been married or had children of her own, she could help the toughest child be good. And so she would not be misunderstood, she told her story every chance she could."

Then Sarah shared her story with Connie Lou the way she had with so many others through the years. She sang sweetly and quietly, as if she were singing a lullaby:

> *Mary let me hold her baby,*
> *Her newborn son.*
> *Though I'd never be a mother,*
> *I felt like one.*
> *Mary let me hold her baby*
> *So she could rest.*
> *Ever since that night I held Him,*
> *My life's been blessed.*

Sarah hummed quietly and rocked the imagined baby in her arms. As she did, John whispered to Constance, "She single-handedly built the largest orphanage in ancient Bethlehem and served there for years. I tried to help her whenever I could."

Constance marveled. "And she never had children of her own?" she asked.

"No one could convince her of that. Every child she met, she loved as her own until the day she died."

"She died? You're telling me this woman's dead?" Constance was whispering too.

"She's just a spirit," John said, keeping his voice low, "but she's doing great work on the other side, I'm told."

"The other side?"

"Of the veil. Sometimes it's very thin, Connie. Sometimes it's very thin."

Sarah sang the final verses of her forgotten carol while rocking the baby she still saw in her arms.

> *Those like me who can't have children*
> *Still can be mothers.*
> *Something in His eyes convinced me*
> *I could serve so many others.*
> *Mary let me hold her baby,*
> *So soft and warm.*
> *Mary let me hold her baby,*
> *And I was reborn.*

"Shhh, he's asleep," Sarah said. Then she walked over to Constance. "You hold him for a while so I can visit with John." Then she placed the swaddling clothes in the nurse's arms and walked into the other room with the old man.

At first Constance thought she would feel silly holding the blanket in the room all alone. But she didn't. Instead, her heart swelled with so much love that she thought it would burst. And for a moment, just a moment, she thought she saw a baby looking up at her from within the swaddling clothes. Without realizing what she was doing, she started to hum Sarah's lullaby.

Then a snowball hit the window. Disoriented, she looked around but saw no one. *I must have dozed off for a few minutes*, she thought. She checked the clock—the time was half past five. She'd been asleep nearly two hours. How embarrassing! How utterly unprofessional!

She hurried to get her things and then called a cab. While she was waiting for it to arrive, something on the Christmas tree caught her eye—an ornament she hadn't seen before. It was a fragment of swaddling cloth tied in the shape of a bow.

CHAPTER 7

A Music Box and an Old Corsage

Halfway home, Constance realized that in her rush to leave, she'd forgotten her clipboard filled with notes and observations about her patient. She probably could have waited to pick it up the next day, but since the hospital was paying the cab fare, she asked the driver to turn around and take her back to the mansion.

When she got to the front door, she decided not to

knock but simply to slip inside. *No need to bother anyone,* she thought. *The butler won't mind, and John's probably asleep anyway.*

She quietly opened the door and tiptoed in. Then she saw Uncle John dancing around the Christmas tree. The music came from a small music box, and the tinkling sound reminded her of something from a Christmas ballet, but it wasn't a tune she recognized. It had an almost bittersweet quality to it.

Constance stayed out of view and watched for a few moments as John continued to dance. He had no partner, of course, but his every gesture, his every glance, made it clear that he was remembering someone very special.

When the music box went silent, he bowed to his imaginary partner, kissed her hand, and took her by the arm to the ornament case. From it he took what looked like a corsage of dried flowers. Then, pantomiming, he pinned it on her. After that, John and his partner danced their way around the room toward the tree. If they were dancing to music, only they could hear it.

During one of his turns, John saw that he was being

watched, and it broke the spell. He just stood there looking at Constance, sad but not angry that the magic of the memory had ended. Constance was about to explain why she had come back and why she entered without knocking, but John spoke first.

"She was my only true love. I have lived long enough to say honestly that I have seen the great beauties of the world, but she was the greatest. Her eyes were windows to a stunningly beautiful soul . . . and she loved me. She saw things in me I couldn't see myself and found a way to bring them out. Over the centuries I have listened as the world's finest composers have tried to capture in music the essence of true love. For other loves they may have succeeded, but for our love, no melody on earth has come close."

He gazed at the corsage of dried flowers in his hand, then went on: "In all these years, the only time I really wished I could die was when she died. Only two things kept me going. One was the fact that she made me promise I'd finish my mission—with honor, no matter what.

The other was the hope that we will be together forever someday.

"I do pretty well the rest of the year. But when I dance our Christmas dance and place her corsage on the tree, I miss her."

There was a loud honk. The cab driver was still waiting. Constance had to go, but with all her heart she wished she could stay with the old man so he wouldn't be alone. Constance never thought of herself as the kind of woman men would find attractive, but she wanted to do something for John—dear, confused John. So she signaled the taxi to wait and then walked over to the music box and wound it up. When it began to play, she stood before her patient and asked, "May I have this dance?"

He pinned the corsage on her crisp white uniform, bowed, took her right hand in his left, and placed his right hand in the small of her back. And then they danced.

It should have been more difficult for Constance than it was. She didn't know how to dance. She could barely remember the last time she had danced, and what a disaster it had been. But this dance wasn't for her—it was for him. She'd been a prisoner to her own concerns, her own insecurities, and her own problems most of her life. But tonight, in the arms of a lonely old man, love was setting her free. Not romantic love. But some kind of love. She'd had so little experience with love in her life that she didn't know what to call it. But the man she was dancing with knew exactly what kind of love it was—pure.

When their dance was over, she unpinned the corsage and placed it on the tree, and then, as she was leaving, paused to kiss Uncle John on the cheek.

As she rode home, she wasn't filled with anxieties about what she'd just done. Even though she'd danced with a patient and kissed him, she didn't feel the slightest guilt or awkwardness or concern. She was at peace. Totally at peace.

As the taxi drove through town, she saw a Christmas banner proclaiming: "PEACE ON EARTH." For the first time in her life, she knew what that meant.

CHAPTER 8

A Heart That
Cannot Hear

*W*hen Constance had finished her dinner and washed the dishes, she sat in her favorite reading chair and just looked around the room. *This room needs something,* she thought. Then she said half aloud, "Maybe I should go out and get a small Christmas tree. It looks kind of drab in here."

When the words left her mouth, the furniture she'd

lived with for so long seemed to cry out in protest. *What are you saying?* the room seemed to ask. *This is what you are. You can't change it! What are you thinking? You can't put up a little tree and disguise who you are. Constance, don't get caught up in your patient's insanity. Be professional. Be competent!*

With this, her peace vanished. Suddenly she felt a knot in her stomach. For Constance there was no greater fear than that of losing the appearance of competency. And she had known that fear since she was fourteen years old. That was the year she was told her mother's latest illness was only temporary. But that had been a lie. Constance watched her mother stoically refuse to accept the truth about her condition—and the truth was, she was dying.

Typically when families receive such news, there's an initial period of denial and anger and heartbreak, followed by a sincere search for tender ways to express deep feelings and say good-bye. But Constance received only her mother's stubborn reassurance that everything was fine and that recovery was just around the corner. In fact, the only thing that even came close to resembling tenderness during that time was something Constance overheard her mother comment to someone on the phone, that the nurse who helped Dr. Burton seemed to be a rather competent woman. It was the nearest thing to a compliment Constance had ever heard her mother give. And so it's probably no surprise that a few years after her mother's death, Constance went into nursing, desperate to prove that she too could be competent. But now she'd failed, and she was sick inside.

She'd gone against her better judgment. She'd allowed a patient to seduce her into his psychosis. She'd lost her professional distance. She'd compromised her professional standards. She'd made no plans for this to happen, but quickly she had to decide what she was going to do. She'd have to tell Mr. Halifax. How humiliating! What would he think? What would become of her? She could lose her job, her world. No, she wouldn't tell anyone, but she'd ask Mr. Halifax to replace her immediately, and she'd fill in at the hospital for whatever nurse he chose. She'd do it in the morning. First thing. *There now. Take a few deep breaths*, she told herself. *That's better. Everything's going to be all right.*

But Constance didn't sleep. Instead, she rehearsed what she would tell Mr. Halifax. She went over and over what she'd say and then how he'd respond. As long and difficult as the night was, there was something familiar about it. It was a bit extreme, perhaps, but the nurse reasoned that this might be what it had taken to bring her back to her senses.

First thing the next morning, she started calling Mr. Halifax, who was always at the office at seven o'clock sharp. But he was already in a meeting. She left both her home number and the phone number at the mansion and pleaded with his secretary to have him return the call as quickly as possible. Between seven o'clock and the time she had to leave to fulfill her duties, she left five messages. She received no call.

As she rode in the cab, she thought things would be much easier if she were in an accident. Everyone would understand then. She wouldn't have to face Uncle John again, and she wouldn't have to explain to Mr. Halifax why she wanted to be excused from her responsibilities. She'd be safely cared for in the hospital she knew so well, with its stark, white, antiseptic walls.

There was no accident, however. She arrived at the home of Uncle John without incident and precisely on time. She paid the cab driver and walked slowly to the door. There was no wonder, no laughter, no childlike anticipation. She was painfully aware of who she was and why she was there.

With dread she rang the front doorbell, and Uncle John immediately opened the door for her.

"Good morning," he said cheerfully. "Sleep well?"

Constance didn't answer.

"You just missed a call from your boss," John informed her. "He said he'd be in meetings most of the day but that he'd try to call you when he had his next break." John seemed to sense that something was wrong. "Connie Lou, are you feeling all right?" he asked with genuine concern.

"I've been better," was all she could say.

"Well, then, I've got just the thing." John was beaming.

"I have an old herbal tea remedy that works every time. I'll have some made up for you right away."

"Please don't bother. I'll be fine." Constance knew that her performance was unconvincing, but it was the best she could do under the circumstances.

"You're worried about something, Connie Lou. It's written all over your face. What is it?"

"It's nothing."

"Is it about last night? Are you feeling awkward about last night?"

How does he always know everything? she wondered. *Can psychotics read minds?*

"Connie Lou, may I tell you something? That was one of the dearest things anyone has ever done for me, as a friend, and one of the most compassionate things you could have done for me as my nurse. And I know compassion. Did I ever tell you about the time I served with Florence Nightingale?"

Constance rolled her eyes. Didn't he *ever* give up?

"Well, some other time, perhaps. I was so touched by what you did for me last night I did something I haven't done in a few hundred years. I made a new ornament to add to my collection." He walked her over to the Christmas tree, then waited for her to discover his creation. Because she didn't know what she was supposed to be looking for, it took her a minute to recognize what Uncle John wanted her to see—the newest ornament on the tree. It was a red cross.

Constance noticed that the ornament had been placed very near the corsage.

"So what's the song that goes with it?" she asked, almost sarcastically.

"Only you can write that one, Connie Lou," he answered.

"But I don't write songs."

"Oh, yes you do," Uncle John said. "We all do. It's just harder for some of us to let them out, that's all."

"Let them out?"

"Out of our hearts," he said. "We may not all be George Frideric Handel, but every meaningful experience we ever have has a song that accompanies it. And we write it in our hearts. Our favorite songs that other people write are the ones that come closest to sounding like the ones we have inside us. And you're writing the one that goes with this ornament right now."

"I'm writing a song . . . right now?" Constance already knew the man was crazy, but he was really proving it now.

"Not consciously, of course. It's all happening inside. And when you're willing to let it be heard, you will discover that just like you, it's beautiful."

Constance just looked at her patient for a long time. She had no words. She was searching for some, but none came. *How do you reason with someone who's lost all touch with reality?* she wondered. *And more important, why am I trying?* He was beyond hope, as far as she could see. He showed no willingness to acknowledge the fact that he was living in a fantasy world. Once again she experienced the irritation she had felt from the beginning.

"Why do you do this?" she asked.

"Do what?"

"Make up all these stories about how long you've lived and the people you've known and how everybody writes songs in their hearts. It's not normal. It's strange. It's not reality. It's not true—"

She had more to say, but Uncle John interrupted her.

"Just a moment. What I've told you may be strange, I grant you that, and it may not be normal or seem real to you, but, as I told you before, I tell the truth."

"Well, I guess all truth is relative," she acknowledged.

John got a bit stern with her for a moment. "Listen, Connie Lou, just because you don't understand something doesn't mean it can't be true. I can respect the fact that you don't believe what I've been telling you, but that doesn't mean it isn't so. The problem with a lot of people who've only been around a few decades is that they cling so tightly to the things they learned yesterday that they can't reach out for the new things that will change their tomorrows."

Uncle John paused. He knew it would take a moment for what he'd said to sink in, and he wanted Constance to think about it before he continued. She did. And then she asked, "But how can you know if something's true when it flies in the face of everything else you think you've learned?"

"That's why we have hearts, Connie Lou. If we'll let them, they are our true teachers. We just have to listen."

"To our *hearts?*" she asked skeptically.

John pointed to the Christmas tree to help make his point. "This season is a perfect example of what I'm talking about. How could anyone even pretend to believe the story of Christmas, if it were not for a willingness to listen to our hearts. Angels singing from the heavens. Stars guiding wise men. A baby born of a virgin who would grow up and save the world . . . come on! Who could possibly believe any of this if there weren't something in our hearts that said, 'Yes, it's true.'

"I met a woman a lot like you who had trouble listening to her heart. But something changed one night when she and I met a carpenter named Joseph."

John began to sing about their experience:

> *He was working late one evening*
> *With the wood he knew so well,*
> *When she thought she recognized him,*

Though at first she couldn't tell.
As she humbly begged his pardon,
A strange sadness swelled inside
When she asked, "Aren't you the father
Of the man they crucified?"

Then the carpenter repeated
What he'd said so many times.
He said, "I was not His father; He was mine."
Then he humbly went on working
With his worn and callused hands.
Though she did not ask more questions,
He knew she did not understand.

And so he asked if she would help him.
He saw her answer in a glance.
And then she did the chores he asked her,
And she felt grateful for the chance.
And then he talked for hours of Jesus,
And how he knew He was divine.
He said, "I was not His father; He was mine.

How could one so foolish and so flawed
Ever hope to raise the Son of God?"
Then he spoke of the misgivings
He had had a thousand times,

And how Jesus found the tender moments
To let him know he'd done just fine.
Then the carpenter recited
The greatest truths he'd ever learned
And testified they came from Jesus.
And then her heart within her burned.

They embraced as she departed,
And Joseph told her one more time,
"Tell them I was not His father;
Tell them He was mine. No, I was
Not His father; He was mine."

John took from his ornament case a small replica of a cradle, which he told Constance looked very much like the one Joseph had built for Jesus. Then he reverently hung it on the tree and turned to Constance.

"In all my years on earth, I have seen time and time again that those who are happiest are those who have the courage to follow their hearts—to believe what otherwise would be unbelievable; to seek the light; to find the truth . . ."

Music entered the room. It was a presence that was very discernible and very real:

Somewhere beneath the glitter
That comes this time of winter,
In many souls there is a cry.
They may not clearly say it,
But in their hearts they pray it.
And you can see it in their eyes.

Constance heard a choir begin to sing, a choir of many, many voices, and for a brief moment she thought she heard her own voice singing with them:

I cannot find my way.
I cannot find my way.
I cannot find my way at all.
There are so many choices,
So many different voices.
I cannot find my way at all.

John ceremoniously took the large star out of the suitcase of ornaments. Constance had never before seen a Christmas ornament so beautiful, and his forgotten carol told the story behind the star:

> *There were three kings who followed the star of*
>   *Bethlehem.*
> *They came from afar to praise and honor Him.*
> *The light which beckoned*
> *Them to seek the Lord of men:*
> *It calls to you,*
> *It calls to me.*

The sound of the choir returned, only fuller this time, as if more voices had joined:

> *We cannot find our way.*
> *We cannot find our way.*
> *We cannot find our way at all.*
> *There are so many choices,*
> *So many different voices.*
> *We cannot find our way at all.*

As if to answer all the voices, John sang more surely and more powerfully than he ever had before:

> *We're not alone;*
> *We have a star that shines today.*
> *The love that He gave teaches how*
> *And shows the way.*

That light is clear to see
If we have faith and believe.
Three kings found the Lord,
And so can we.

The choir sang counter to John:

We cannot find our way.
We cannot find our way at all.

But John confidently repeated his claim:

Three kings found the Lord, and so can we.
And if you've lost your way,
That light burns bright today.
And it will shine eternally.
Three kings found the Lord,
And so can we.
Three kings found the Lord,
And so can we.
Three kings found the Lord,
And so must we.

The strength of John's forgotten carol overwhelmed
the voices of despair and confusion, and the choir began
to sing:

Lord, help us find our way.
We need to find our way.
Lord, help us find our way back home.

Constance heard her own voice joining in, and for the first time since her dance the night before, she felt harmony in her soul. So when John invited Constance to place the star at the top of the tree, she willingly agreed.

To reach the top, she would need a stepladder, so John went to get one for her. While he was gone, she got a chance to study the star more carefully. She noticed a pearl in its very center, framed by four indentations. Three of those were filled with what looked like a ruby, an emerald, and a sapphire. The fourth indentation was empty. When John returned with the ladder, he explained that the pearl at the center represented the Lord, and the three gems represented the three kings who sought Him, found Him, and honored Him. The empty space, he told her, was for all of us who needed to follow their example.

John then steadied the ladder as Constance placed the crowning ornament on the tree. She wanted it to be perfect, so she asked John to step back a few feet and let her know if it looked straight. When a knock came at the front door, John excused himself to answer it. Constance wondered where the butler was when they needed him.

From her vantage point on the ladder, she couldn't clearly see or hear everything that was happening in the entry, but what she did hear frightened her. She caught little pieces of phrases: "You'll have to come with us. . . . Did you really think you could get away with this again? . . . You have the right to remain silent . . ."

Constance went numb for a moment, frozen on the ladder. She didn't know what to do. After a moment or two, a policeman entered the living room and saw Constance on the stepladder looking a bit like a kitten caught in a tree.

"You must be the nurse from the hospital," he said a little gruffly.

"What are you doing here? What's going on, officer?" she called down to him.

"The neighbors called us because they knew the family

95

was on vacation in Europe and were concerned that strangers were in the house."

"But this is his house! He's their uncle, and I'm here at their request, caring for him."

"I've got to hand it to the man. He's clever. But he's done this before and kind of gave himself away this time. Don't you want to get down from there?" he asked, and Constance obeyed.

"What do you mean he's done this before, officer?"

"A couple of years ago in Granville, a lonely old man sent a wire to a nearby hospital saying that if they would send a nurse to care for the family's aging uncle while they were in Europe, there was a good chance they'd get some kind of donation when they returned."

Constance turned as white as the snow outside. "What happened?" she asked.

"Well, from what the Granville sheriff told us, he didn't hurt anybody or steal anything. In fact, the crazy old coot even gave some money to the hospital."

"So why did he do it?"

"Huh! Who knows? Maybe he didn't want to spend

Christmas alone." The officer shook his head. "Look, I'll need you to come down to the station with me for some routine questioning, and then we'll let you go. Sorry for the inconvenience."

"What's going to happen to him?" she asked.

"He's probably homeless or senile. We'll let him spend a night or two at the jail until we can find out if he's got any relatives. Then, if no charges are pressed against him, we'll try to find an institution that will take him."

Constance gathered her things and rode to the county jail with the officer. He talked on his police radio most of the ride, but Constance didn't hear much of what he was saying; she was lost in a world of her own. At first she was in shock. Then she tried to put the pieces together. And then she became angry—angry at John for playing such a cruel practical joke on her. Maybe it wasn't meant to be a joke on her, but it was. She felt used, deceived, taken advantage of. And the more she thought about it, the angrier she became.

After arriving at the station and answering a few questions and giving her statement, she asked if she could see

John before she left. She didn't tell the officer why, but she wanted to give John, or whatever his name was, a piece of her mind. While she waited to see if a final meeting with her "patient" could be arranged, she called the hospital, trying to get through to Mr. Halifax, but he could not be reached. She decided that any message she might leave would only confuse him, since she was still confused herself, so she left word she'd talk to him in the morning.

It took some doing, but the officer arranged for her to have a few minutes with John before taking him away. "Would you like to have me there as a protection?" he asked her.

"For me or for him?" she asked, and she saw a sly grin come over the officer's face.

"Well, you both look pretty harmless to me. But in case you have a problem, just holler. I'll be right outside the room."

She entered the cubicle where John was sitting and stood in front of him. She wasn't planning on sitting down. She was going to tell him a thing or two and then make a dramatic exit. Since she hadn't really had time to plan what she was going to say or do, she had no idea what would happen. But she didn't care about any of that. She just wanted to let the volcano that was churning inside her erupt.

"Well, Mr. *Truth,* this must be a little awkward for you," she began. "Just when you had me right where you wanted me, someone pulled back the curtain, and there you stood, like the mighty Wizard of Oz, revealed as the fraud and scam artist you are. Tell me, is it exciting to play with someone's heart and mind? Does it give you a feeling of power?"

John sat listening, quietly and somehow understandingly. "I wasn't playing."

"You *weren't?* Then *what did you think you were doing?*" Constance was stunned to hear herself shouting at the old man. It frightened her because she didn't know what else would come out, and she couldn't stop it.

"You took advantage of me. I don't know how, but you knew my weaknesses, my vulnerabilities. Just like my mother, you manipulated my emotions, as a sculptor

99

molds his clay. Only you made me into something I didn't want to be." As the words poured out, so did her tears. "You made me something I didn't want to be! *And then you left me—you lied to me and then you left!*" She was sobbing inconsolably. "I *hate* you for hurting me . . ."

John reached out to comfort her. "Don't touch me, Mother. . . . I'm furious with you . . ." Her words lingered in the air and mingled with the sound of her crying. A flood of hurt poured out and then buried itself in John's shoulder. As she wept, he gently stroked her hair and whispered, "Let it all out, Connie Lou. Let it all out."

As much as she ached, she was beginning to feel cleansed somehow, as if she were washing out an infection from the deepest part of her soul. When the reservoir of tears was empty and she finally began to breathe normally, John held her by the shoulders and made her look at him.

"You can start to heal now, Connie Lou," he said tenderly.

CHAPTER 9

The Carol in Her Heart

The guard came in to take John away. Constance wanted a few more minutes, but she couldn't have them. John asked her for a favor. "Could you get my ornaments for me . . . please?" he said, and then he was gone.

Constance didn't know if she could do what he asked her. She didn't know if the ornaments were some sort of evidence she wasn't supposed to touch, so she asked the officer if it was all right to return to the house and collect the ornaments along with the rest of John's things. He smiled and said he'd arrange for someone to take her.

On the ride back to the mansion, Constance planned what she would do. She'd first check to see if John's clothes, his flute, and the shepherd's costume were upstairs in his room. Then she'd get his ornament case, place it near the tree, and then put the ornaments all back in the antique suitcase that carried them. By the time she'd made these plans and had a few mental reviews for possible problems, the police car pulled into the mansion's driveway.

Returning to the house knowing that John wouldn't be there was odd. She wondered if the butler would be bumbling around somewhere. Immediately upon entering, she set out to execute her plan, first going upstairs to see if anything was left in John's room, wherever that was. At the top of the stairs she saw a hall with several doors, but since only one was open, she thought she'd try there first.

On the bed were some things she expected to see—

and a few she didn't. John's sweater was there. And his shepherd's clothing. And his flute. But next to the flute was a wig and a beard, thick glasses, some padding, and the clothes she had seen the butler wear—in those few glimpses she'd had of him. She was surprised, but then again, she wasn't that surprised the more she thought about it.

Her greatest surprise came when she went downstairs and collected the old Christmas ornament suitcase. When she picked it up to move it closer to the tree, a flap inside the lid fell open, and out spilled several newspaper articles and an envelope. In the envelope was a cashier's check made out to Regional Hospital for five thousand dollars. Not exactly a major endowment, but it was a promised gift nonetheless. Constance wondered where a man like John could have come up with the money. She hoped it wasn't stolen.

The newspaper articles were in various shades of aging yellow, but the headlines carried similar themes. One article from the *Granville Gazette* in December of 1969 was cleverly headlined:

DECK THE HALLS WITH BOUGHS OF FOLLY
It appears that Santa isn't the only one who
sneaks into people's houses to surprise them at
Christmastime. Last week, in the suburb of . . .

The article went on to explain what the officer had
told her—that John "borrowed" the homes of wealthy
people who were away during the holidays and then
arranged for a nurse to spend those few days "caring" for
him in exchange for a promised but unspecified gift.
Constance didn't like the article because the tone was
too facetious. She picked up another. This one, dated
December 27, 1964, came from a small-town paper in
Missouri:

BUTCHER CLAIMS CON MAN
TAUGHT HIM FORGOTTEN CAROLS
A local butcher claims that a mysterious
customer taught him Christmas carols about
forgotten parts of the Christian holiday . . .

Though the article wasn't about a nurse, Constance

recognized unmistakable similarities to what had happened to her.

She read article after article in newspapers from all across North America: Dec. 10th, 1951, NEW YORK FAMILY CLAIMS THEY HAD THEIR OWN MIRACLE ON 34th STREET. Uncle John had really been around. *He must have been fairly young when he started doing this*, she thought when she read the article from the *Des Moines Register* of December 1932.

HOLIDAY HOPE DOWNTOWN

"With so many out of work this holiday season, many gather at the Main Street soup kitchen for food and 'Forgotten Carols.' Recipients say an elderly out-of-towner affectionately called Uncle John gives hope to the homeless."

The farther back Constance read, the more she marveled that no matter what year the article was written, the desciptions of Uncle John were all the same. It would appear he was ageless. But how could he be?

One of the articles at the bottom of the pile caught

Connie Lou's attention because for some reason it had been preserved in a plastic bag. It was from *The Stars and Stripes*, dated January 5th 1943. It read: "REMOTE MASH UNIT NOT FORGOTTEN: It seems the USO didn't know there was an eccentric entertainer visiting remote units on Christmas eve with peaceful music and unusual stories. 'You never expect to meet someone like John in a place like this,' said Lieutenant James Preston Chamberlain."

Constance paused, and read the words out loud to make sure she'd read them correctly. "Said Lieutenant James Preston Chamberlain." As she heard herself speak her father's name, a strangely familiar, warm feeling came over her, and she read on:

"'There was something in those forgotten Christmas carols that gave the season a whole new meaning for me. Perhaps it was the magic in the air.'"

She stood up, as if she were about to meet someone for the first time, though no one was there. She held the newspaper article with a tenderness reserved for very precious things. As she did, she imagined her father's face, only known to her through pictures, reacting to each of John's carols. She wished she could have been there, seen them together, listened to them talk. She wondered if her father spoke to John of the child his wife was carrying, and what her name might be. The more she thought about the connection between her father and Uncle John, the more she realized that this Christmas was not an accident, it was a gift.

Constance carefully returned the articles to their special compartment in the suitcase and reported to the officer, who was on the phone in the other room, about the cashier's check to the hospital. Then she proceeded to take the ornaments off the tree. As she held each one, she was enveloped in the memories and the melodies that accompanied them. She rediscovered the significance and meaning of each one: the star; the cradle; the bow made of swaddling clothes; the corsage of dried flowers; the composer's pen; the shepherd's flute; the entrance to the inn. All filled her heart again as she laid them in their appointed places in the leather and wood case.

There wasn't a place for the newest ornament in the

collection—the red cross. And no melody came quickly to her mind as she held it. But one was there, buried in her heart, and without her knowing how it happened, suddenly it was set free.

I thought I'd seen all the lights and sung all the songs.
I felt the holiday lasted a bit too long.
I never shed any tears
When Christmas was through,
Until I celebrated one with you. And now
I cry the day that I take the tree down.
I want the season to last all year round.
When I'm surrounded by these memories,
It's almost like you're here with me.

As she sang, she also danced with a partner who wasn't there. Had anyone been watching, they'd have noticed that every gesture, every glance, every movement made it clear that whoever she was remembering was someone very special.

It's strange how things are changed
When touched by love.
We treasure things we never thought much of.

I cry the day that I take the tree down.
And I want the season to last all year round.
And I am dreaming of Christmases when
We'll be together again.

She could hardly finish the song for the tears. She'd never cried tears like that before. They were cleansing tears that carried a lifetime of unexpressed feelings. They were tears of love lost and love found. They were tears of understanding of all she had missed, and tears of gratitude for all she could now receive. When she had cried them all out, she felt reborn.

Oh, how she wished that John could have heard her carol—the one he had told her she was writing in her heart. Of all the people in the world, he was the one she most wanted to share it with. *Perhaps I'll have that chance when I return his ornaments*, she thought.

Not knowing whether to keep her red cross or to place it in the case, she decided at length to place it with the other ornaments. She felt that it would be a unique honor to have something of herself in such company.

CHAPTER 10

In His Love There Is a Home

When Constance returned to the jail, searching for the officer in charge, she was distracted by the sound of singing down the hall, and the tune was hauntingly familiar. It sounded as though it might be coming from one of the jail cells. When she focused on the singing long enough to understand the words, she recognized it as the Christmas carol she'd heard before, sung by a group

of singers huddled around a fire that was burning in a
garbage can painted like a Christmas tree:

> *Homeless, homeless*
> *Like the Christ child was . . . we are*
> *Homeless, homeless,*
> *But there is hope because . . .*

A uniformed policeman interrupted her listening and
asked if she needed any help.

"I'm here to see the old man." She said. "I have something for him."

"Oh, the choir director." The officer smiled and nodded toward the singing down the hall. "It's our very own
Jailernacle Choir. He wasn't here twenty minutes before
he had 'em learning harmony. I'm gonna miss that guy."

"Miss him? You mean he's gone? How could he be
gone?" she asked.

"Somebody bailed him out an hour ago. It was a
woman. I think her name was Sarah."

Constance responded with absolute certainty. "It
couldn't possibly have been Sarah."

"Why not?"

"Because she died nineteen hundred years ago!!!" As the words came out of her mouth she realized they would need more of an explanation than she cared to give, so she quickly tried to change the subject. "Just tell me where he's gone so I can get these ornaments to him."

"Sorry, lady. All he left was a note for some person named Connie Lou."

Constance held out her hand "That's me . . . sort of."

The policeman handed her an envelope that Constance quietly opened and read in the hallway that led to the jail.

My Dearest Connie Lou,
Thanks so much for every-
thing. You'll never know how
much knowing you has
enriched my life. I also
want you to have the orna-
ments as my Christmas present
to you. After so many years

of traveling, I feel they need a permanent home, and I can't think of a more perfect one than yours. And, Connie Lou, I too am dreaming of Christmases when we'll be together again.

Merry Christmas,

John

He had heard her song, her forgotten carol. He had heard it long before she knew it had been written in her heart. She tenderly pressed the note against her chest. She rocked back and forth and found herself singing something totally unpredictable but completely true.

All I ever wanted, all I ever dreamed of,
Everything I hoped, and all the things I prayed for,
Couldn't hold a candle to what I've been given;
I've been given what I need.
A mansion on a hill or love like in the movies,
Perfect little lives where no one has a problem,

Instead of all those things I thought I really wanted,
I've been given what I need.
Even when I didn't understand,
When I thought you had no heart,
Thank you for rejecting my demands
And always giving me the better part.
'Cause all I ever wanted, all I ever dreamed of,
Everything I hoped and all the things I prayed for
Couldn't hold a candle to what I've been given;
I've been given what I need.

The next morning, Constance got a chance to tell Mr. Halifax what had happened, and she presented him with the check for five thousand dollars. She prevented him from acting disappointed over the amount by spouting the virtues he himself had espoused at every telethon he'd ever appeared on in behalf of the hospital: "Your contribution, of even a few dollars," she half impersonated his delivery, "will be a living, working legacy here at Regional Hospital." She silently dared him to say anything critical after that.

Then she informed him that she'd like to work Christmas day and give some of the other nurses a chance to be with their families. She surprised him again when she asked if she could help in the maternity ward. She made sure she was scheduled, and then she left his office.

On Christmas day, there were three glorious miracles: three new babies came into the world, and Constance was there to help deliver all three. During one of her breaks, she just watched the joyful fathers and mothers marvel at their newborn children. Later that day, one of the fathers recognized the nurse who had helped with the delivery of his baby and approached her.

"You were there, weren't you? Delivering babies? Well, you've probably delivered lots of babies, but you might remember ours . . . we had the really pretty one." The new father could barely contain his excitement. "I want to thank you, so much. When things got crazy in there you knew just what to do. Like the part where we were doing that Lamaze thing during the contractions. Somebody should have told me that doesn't work that great. But when my wife started screamin', you knew just what to do and how to calm her down. You were so . . .

so . . . competent. Anyway, I know I'm rambling, but this is Christmas day and you probably wanted to be home with your family, but you were helping us welcome a new member to ours. I'm just so grateful for everything, and I wanted to wish you a Merry Christmas, Ms. . . . Ms. . . ." He struggled to see her name tag, but it was covered by a blanket she had over her shoulder.

"My name is Constance," she said almost automatically. But she paused. And as she looked into the eyes of the young father, his sweetness reminded her of a dear friend. A friend she would try to tell others about every Christmas for the rest of her life, a friend she could only describe as . . . *beloved*.

"My name is Constance," she smiled, "but my friends . . . all my friends call me Connie Lou."

Epilogue

*F*lash forward several years. Nurse Chamberlain is a different woman than she was before she cared for the mysterious patient who liked to be called Uncle John. The impact of that encounter has become more pronounced each and every Christmas. This particular year Nurse Chamberlain has had a busy holiday season. She's been in charge of the Regional Hospital Christmas pageant, which she has written, produced, directed, AND choreographed. She's enlisted the talents of the local high school band and chorus, the choirs of two neighboring churches, and a group of harmonizing homeless guys looking for a record deal.

Constance has been amazed how many songs she's discovered in her heart since she met her all-time favorite patient. In fact, Connie Lou has recorded her own collection of Christmas carols, some forgotten, some not, and a new one she just discovered this year. The proceeds from her album will buy Christmas gifts for all the children spending the holidays in her hospital.

As this year's pageant comes to a close, Connie Lou confidently, and competently, takes center stage. She's wearing her crisp, white nurse's uniform with red trim and a fuzzy red-and-white Santa cap. She carries a sleigh bell, which she shakes to get everyone's attention.

"I just want to thank everyone who has made this year's program the best ever. This year's theme, LET THE LIGHT OF THE SEASON LIGHT THE WORLD, is one I hope we'll use for years to come." Connie Lou then

nods to the conductor and the musicians prepare to
accompany her as she sings:

He did not come in glory when He first came to earth
And most the world ignored His humble birth.
But the heavens were singing in celestial harmonies
And a star guided some souls to their knees—
Those with ears to hear and eyes to see.

And the miracles followed but the skeptics believed
They were lies spread by those who'd been deceived.
With their appetite for power they mocked every word He
* said,*
While the ones truly hungering, He fed.
Those who hungered after righteousness were fed.

And the light that He gave
Was to lift and to save,
And the burdens that He came to bear
Are the ones we can't carry
And need to share.

I give thanks for His sweetness, I have faith in His power,
And I know He'll strive with me every hour—
For He suffered in darkness kneeling in Gethsemane

So the light of His love could shine on me.
So the light of His love could shine through me.

Arise! Arise!!
Let's all arise.
Brothers and sisters arise—
Arise and shine forth let us add to the flame
That burns brightly in hearts that bear His name
And the torch that's a standard
For the nations all to see
Is the Light of the World shining through me.

We are standing for something, prayerful in all things,
Comforting those that mourn.
We are gathering Zion, we can rely on this refuge from
    the storm.
We are strengthened on every side
In the light that we cannot hide.
We are united, spirits ignited, feeling the fire inside.

Arise and shine forth and we'll add to the flame
That burns brightly in hearts that bear His name.
And this torch that's a standard for the nations all to see
Is the Light of the World that shines in you and me.
It's the Light of the World
Shining through me.